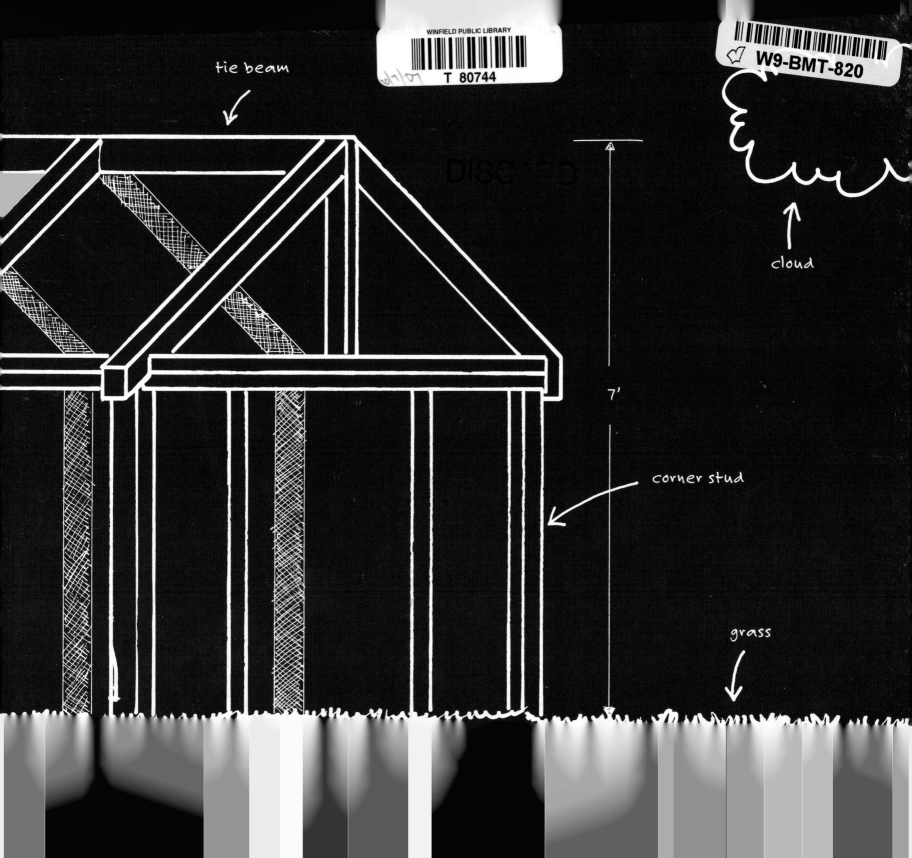

LET'S BUILD
— A —
CLUBHOUSE

by **Marilyn Singer**   Illustrated by **Timothy Bush**

CLARION BOOKS/New York

Clarion Books
a Houghton Mifflin Company imprint
215 Park Avenue South, New York, NY 10003
Text copyright © 2006 by Marilyn Singer
Illustrations copyright © 2006 by Timothy Bush

The illustrations were executed in watercolor.

www.clarionbooks.com

Printed in China

Library of Congress Cataloging-in-Publication Data
Singer, Marilyn.
Let's build a clubhouse / by Marilyn Singer ; illustrated by Timothy Bush.
p. cm.
Summary: Rhyming text describes how a group of children works
together to build a clubhouse, using a variety of tools.
Includes facts about each tool and its use.
ISBN-13: 978-0-618-30670-1
ISBN-10: 0-618-30670-6
[1. Tools—Fiction. II. Carpentry—Fiction. III. Cooperativeness—Fiction.
IV. Clubhouses—Fiction. V. Stories in rhyme.] I. Bush, Timothy, ill. II. Title.
PZ8.3.S6154Let 2006
[E]—dc22
2005030085

WKT 10 9 8 7 6 5 4 3 2 1

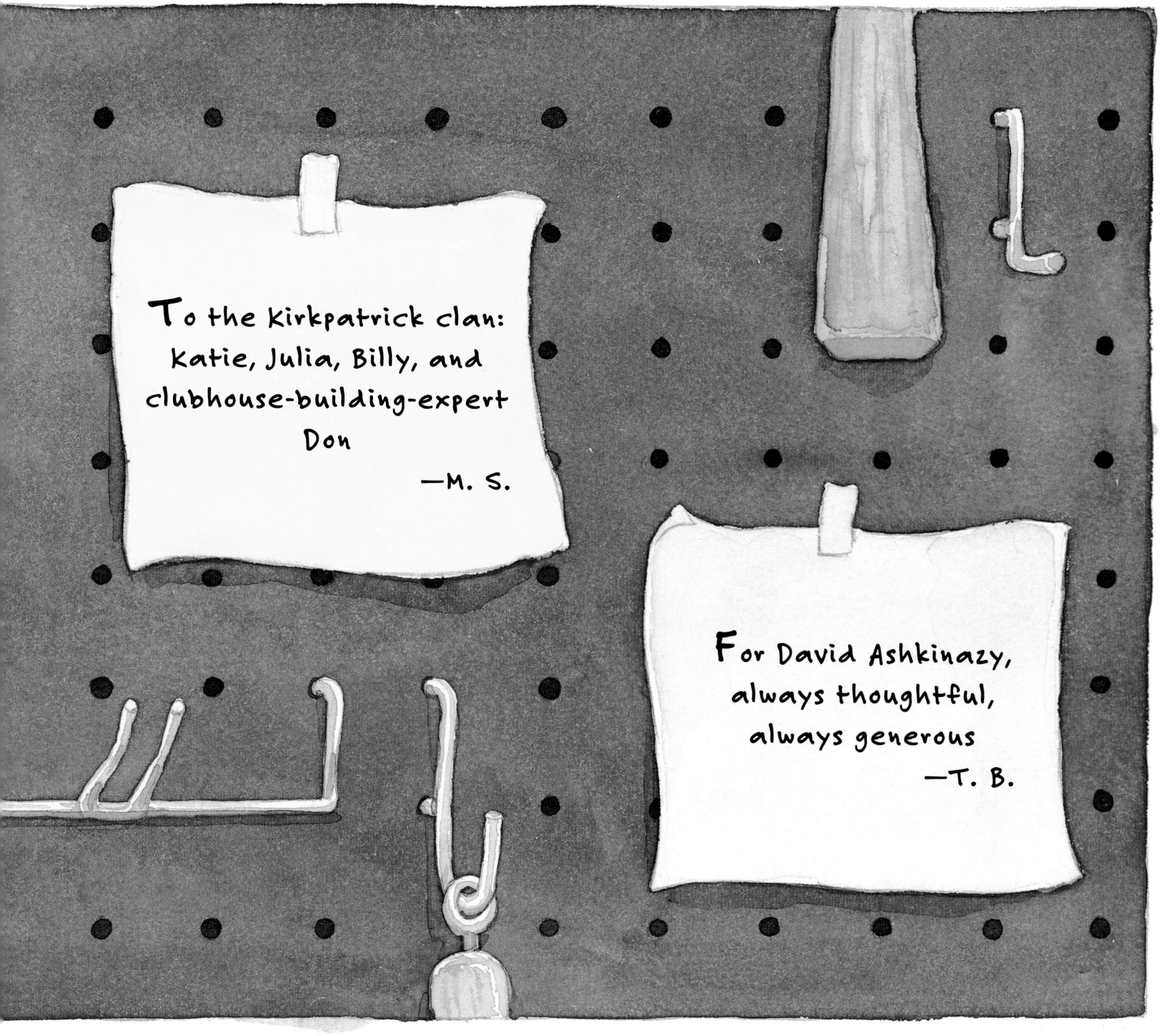
To the Kirkpatrick clan:
Katie, Julia, Billy, and
clubhouse-building-expert
Don
—M. S.
For David Ashkinazy,
always thoughtful,
always generous
—T. B.

Let's build a clubhouse,
a place where we can hide.
Eight feet long
and six feet wide.

Let's build a clubhouse
with windows and shelves.
Let's find the tools
to make it ourselves.

Who's got the plan?

Daniel's got the plan.

A plan is a picture of the shape and the scale
and the building's details, so the builders won't fail!

Before you can build a clubhouse, you need a drawing that shows the design and the measurements. You need a plan.

Who's got the ruler?

Julia's got the ruler.

TOOLS &
MATERIALS

1   2   3   4   5   6

8

With a ruler you can measure a window or door.
You can measure the ceiling. You can measure the floor.

1 ft. = 12 in.
1 yd. = 3 ft.

Rulers measure length, width, height, and depth. They are usually 6 or 12 inches long.
Folding rulers are 6 feet long. Measuring tapes can unroll and stretch from 6 to 100 feet.

7   8   9   10   11   12   13   14   15   16

Who's got the saw?

Lola's got the saw.

A saw's sharp teeth are zip-zaw good

at making two pieces out of one piece of wood.

HANDSAWS   COMPASS SAW   COPING SAW

All handsaws have a handle and a metal blade with sharp teeth for cutting wood and other materials. Different sizes of teeth and different blades make different kinds of cuts.

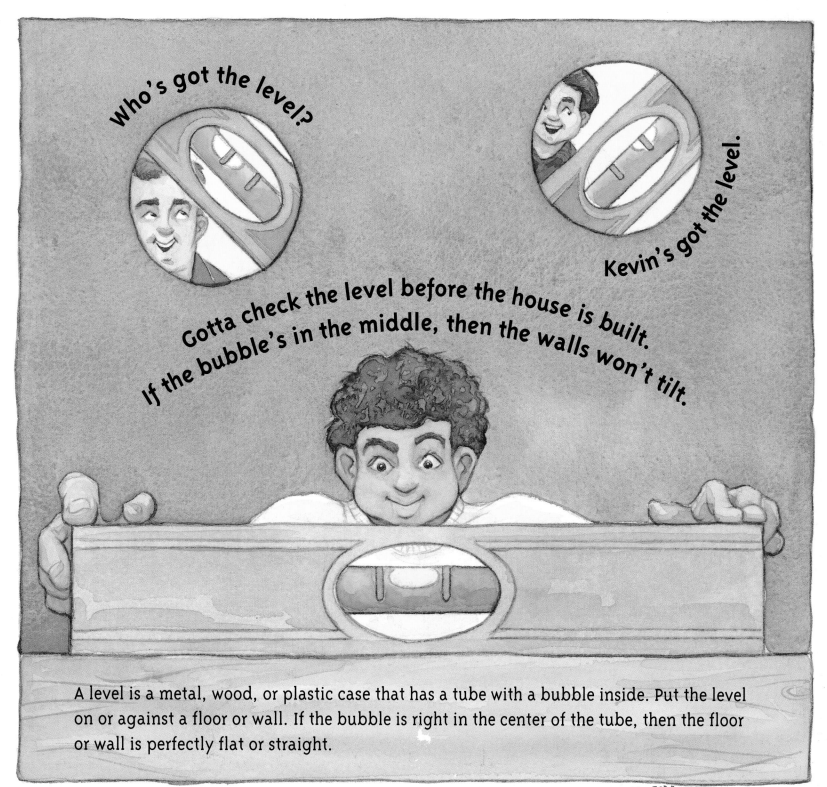

A level is a metal, wood, or plastic case that has a tube with a bubble inside. Put the level on or against a floor or wall. If the bubble is right in the center of the tube, then the floor or wall is perfectly flat or straight.

Who's got the square?

Claire's got the square.

Take a carpenter's square
when you have to create
a line that's perfect for
a cut that's straight.

A carpenter's square is really a *right angle*—half a rectangle. It not only helps you draw straight lines, it can also tell you if the corners you've made are neat or crooked.

Who's got the wrench?

Billy's got the wrench.

A wrench can tighten every bolt and nut
to make a sturdy floor from the boards you cut.

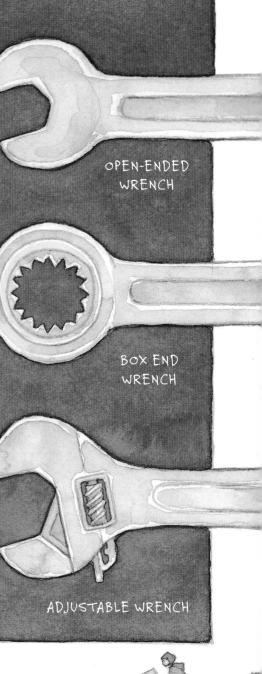

OPEN-ENDED
WRENCH

BOX END
WRENCH

ADJUSTABLE WRENCH

Every builder needs wrenches to hold and tighten nuts and bolts.
Some wrenches have open ends, like jaws. Others have *box,* or
closed, ends. Some wrenches have both.

Who's got the hammer?

Sam's got the hammer.

Take a hammer, take a nail, and then you pound.
Join those pieces of wood with a *wham! bam!* sound.

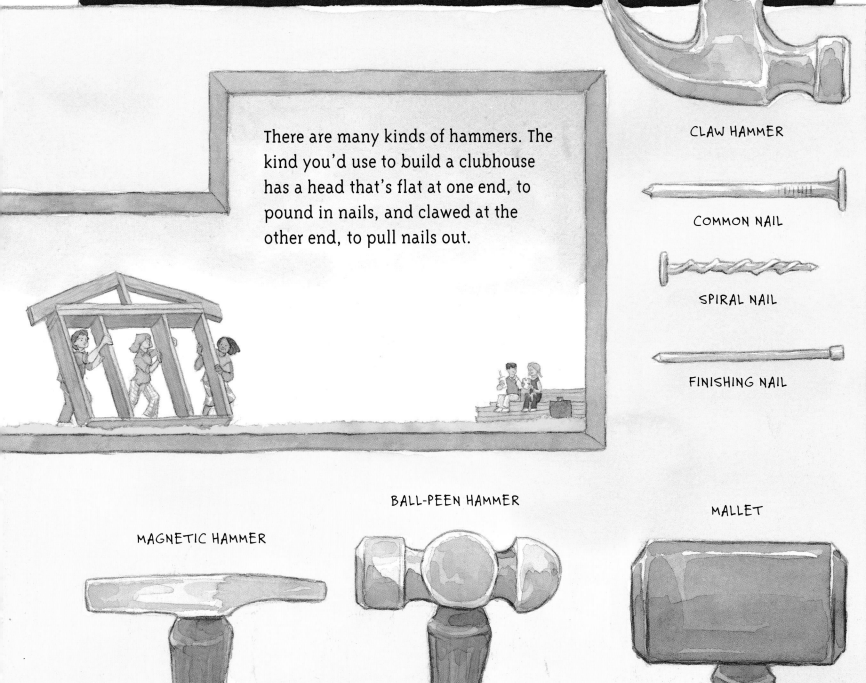

There are many kinds of hammers. The kind you'd use to build a clubhouse has a head that's flat at one end, to pound in nails, and clawed at the other end, to pull nails out.

CLAW HAMMER

COMMON NAIL

SPIRAL NAIL

FINISHING NAIL

MAGNETIC HAMMER

BALL-PEEN HAMMER

MALLET

TWIST BIT

3/8

1/2

1

SPADE BITS

HOLE SAW
BIT

Who's got the drill? Lily's got the drill.

A whiz-biz drill has just one goal—
never quit till the bit
makes the right-sized hole.

Before you use a screw, you first have to make a hole in the wood with a drill. The drill uses a twisted tip called a *bit* to bore the opening. The bigger the bit, the bigger the hole.

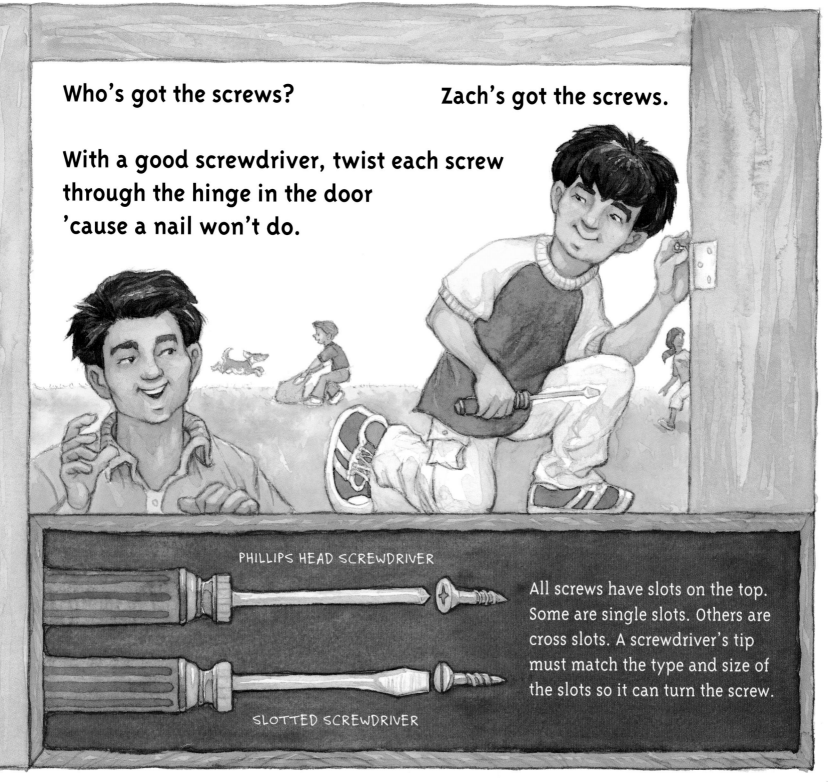

Who's got the screws?

Zach's got the screws.

With a good screwdriver, twist each screw through the hinge in the door 'cause a nail won't do.

PHILLIPS HEAD SCREWDRIVER

SLOTTED SCREWDRIVER

All screws have slots on the top. Some are single slots. Others are cross slots. A screwdriver's tip must match the type and size of the slots so it can turn the screw.

Who's got the plane?

Elena's got the plane.

A plane shaves wood when it's just too thick.
Try its scrape-shape trick and your door won't stick.

A plane is a sharp blade in a case of wood or metal.
Push the plane carefully to shave off curls of wood.
Keep checking to find out when the board or door
fits right and is smooth to the touch.

Who's got the brush?

Tasha's got the brush.

Dip the brush in the paint.

Slap the walls.

Make a sign.

Now this clubhouse

is yours and mine!

We've built a clubhouse,
a place where we can hide.
Eight feet long and six feet wide.
Six feet wide and seven feet tall.

And we did it with teamwork—
the best tool of all!

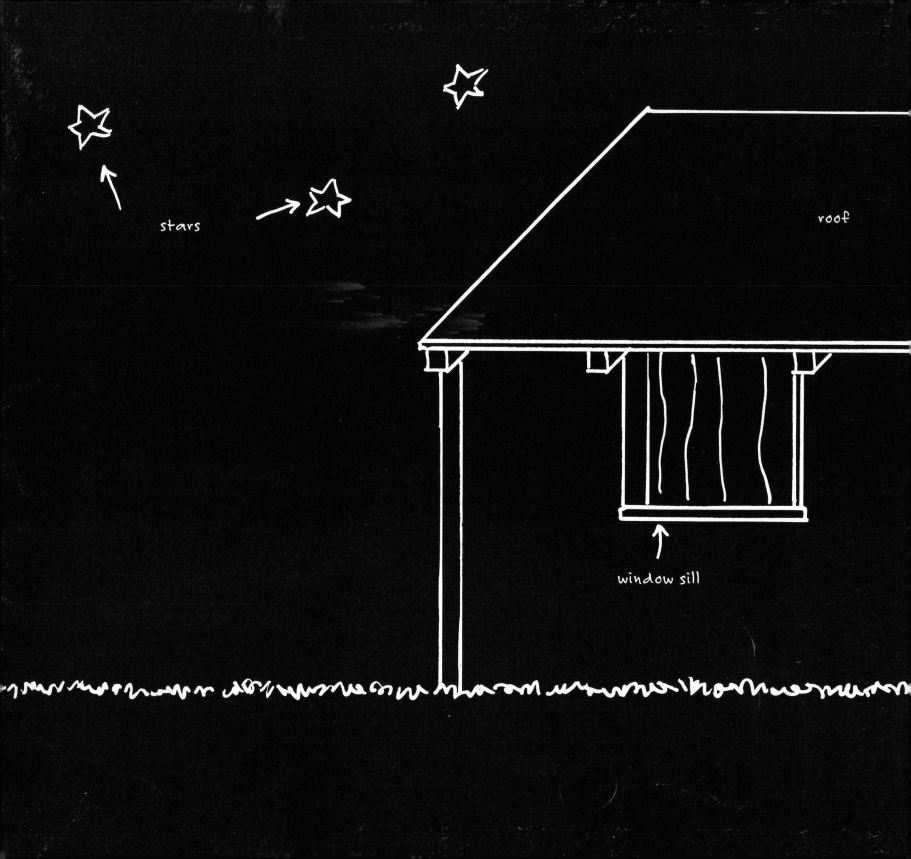